Welcome to ALADDIN QUIX!

If you are looking for fast, fun-to-read stories with colorful characters, lots of kid-friendly humor, easy-to-follow action, entertaining story lines, and lively illustrations, then **ALADDIN QUIX** is for you!

But wait, there's more!

If you're also looking for stories with tables of contents; word lists; about-the-book questions; 64, 80, or 96 pages; short chapters; short paragraphs; and large fonts, then **ALADDIN QUIX** is *definitely* for you!

ALADDIN QUIX: The next step between ready to reads and longer, more challenging chapter books, for readers five to eight years old.

Read more ALADDIN QUIX books!

By Stephanie Calmenson

Our Principal Is a Frog!
Our Principal Is a Wolf!
Our Principal's in His Underwear!
Our Principal Breaks a Spell!

A Miss Mallard Mystery
By Robert Quackenbush

Dig to Disaster
Texas Trail to Calamity
Express Train to Trouble
Stairway to Doom
Bicycle to Treachery
Gondola to Danger
Surfboard to Peril
Taxi to Intrigue
Cable Car to Catastrophe
Dogsled to Dread
Stage Door to Terror

Little Goddess Girls
By Joan Holub and Suzanne Williams

Book 1: *Athena & the Magic Land*
Book 2: *Persephone & the Giant Flowers*
Book 3: *Aphrodite & the Gold Apple*

MACK RHINO
PRIVATE EYE'

The Big Race Lace Case

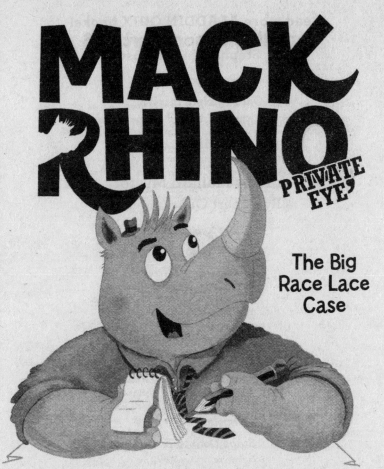

BY PAUL DUBOIS JACOBS AND JENNIFER SWENDER
ILLUSTRATED BY KARL WEST

Q QUIX

ALADDIN QUIX

New York London Toronto Sydney New Delhi

For all the moose at SES

This book is a work of fiction. Any references to historical events, real people, or real places are used fictitiously. Other names, characters, places, and events are products of the author's imagination, and any resemblance to actual events or places or persons, living or dead, is entirely coincidental.

ALADDIN QUIX

Simon & Schuster Children's Publishing Division

1230 Avenue of the Americas, New York, New York 10020

This Aladdin QUIX paperback edition January 2020

Text copyright © 2020 by Jennifer Swender and Paul DuBois Jacobs

Illustrations copyright © 2020 by Karl West

Also available in an Aladdin QUIX hardcover edition.

All rights reserved, including the right of reproduction in whole or in part in any form.

ALADDIN and the related marks and colophon are trademarks of Simon & Schuster, Inc.

For information about special discounts for bulk purchases, please contact

Simon & Schuster Special Sales at 1-866-506-1949 or business@simonandschuster.com.

The Simon & Schuster Speakers Bureau can bring authors to your live event. For more information or to book an event contact the Simon & Schuster Speakers Bureau at 1-866-248-3049 or visit our website at www.simonspeakers.com.

Book designed by Tiara Iandiorio

The illustrations for this book were rendered digitally.

The text of this book was set in Archer Medium.

Manufactured in the United States of America 1219 OFF

2 4 6 8 10 9 7 5 3 1

Library of Congress Control Number 2019936830

ISBN 978-1-5344-4113-2 (hc)

ISBN 978-1-5344-4112-5 (pbk)

ISBN 978-1-5344-4114-9 (eBook)

Cast of Characters

Mack Rhino, Private Eye: a detective

Redd Oxpeck: Mack's trusted assistant

Queenie Zee: Mack and Redd's friend; owner of Queenie's Cupcakes

Ant Hill Gang: a group of sneaky ants

Terry Berry: Mack and Redd's friend; owner of Terry Berry's Smoothie Shack

Jackie Rabbit: a runner in the Big Race and a favorite to win

Skunks McGee: a runner in the Big Race who doesn't play fair

Surfer Jo: A surfer on Beach Street

Lifeguard Sally: A local lifeguard

Juggling Jenkins Twins: Two kids who live on Beach Street

Daisy: Mack and Redd's friend; owner of Daisy's Blossom Barn

Contents

Crash!

Snug in his office at Number 21 Beach Street, **Mack Rhino, Private Eye**, rolled up the blinds and rolled up his sleeves.

For cases big or small, Mack Rhino, Private Eye, was your guy.

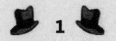

Or . . . rhino.

Mack poured himself a mug of chocolate milk. He took out his notebook. He **reviewed** his list.

Blinds √
Sleeves √
Chocolate milk √

He sat down to start his day.

CRASH!

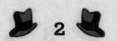

For the third time that month, Mack Rhino had squashed his desk chair.

"Not again." **Redd Oxpeck**, his trusted assistant, giggled.

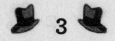

Mack picked up his notebook. He added this to his list:

> Get a rhino-proof chair.

In spite of the broken chair, Mack was in a good mood. He and Redd had just solved their ninety-ninth case.

Case #99—A Picnic Fit for a Queenie—was a real **humdinger**.

A fancy picnic had been stolen from **Queenie Zee**, owner of Queenie's Cupcakes.

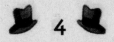 4

Mack and Redd only had a few crumbs to go by, but they didn't have to look far. This case had the **Ant Hill Gang** written all over it.

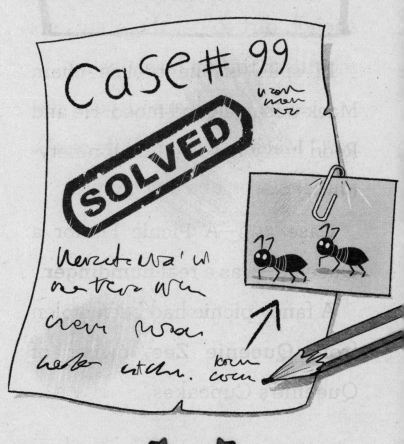

Too bad the ants ate most of the **evidence**. Mack didn't even get one of Queenie's famous cupcakes. Still, Mack and Redd dug up enough dirt to get those ants six months at the ant farm upstate.

"I hope you learned your lesson," Mack told them. "Life on the ant farm won't be any picnic."

Shoes and Clues

"What's the plan for today, Boss?" asked Redd.

"First stop," said Mack. "Fifi's Fine Furniture. I need a new chair."

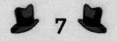

"Let's hurry!" said Redd. "I want to be back in time for the finish of the Big Race."

The Big Race was the biggest event of the year in Coral Cove. Runners came from far and wide

to **compete**. The grand prize was quite a few clams, which meant a lot of money!

The racecourse **snaked** through the park, past the library, and around the school. Then it ran

straight down Beach Street to the finish line.

Mack tucked his notebook into his pocket. But before he could step out the door—

Ring-ring. Ring-ring.

Mack picked up the phone. "Mack Rhino, Private Eye. For cases big or small, I'm your guy. Or . . . rhino."

"I need your help," said a voice. **"And fast!"**

"Case #100," said Mack. "What seems to be the problem?"

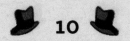

"It's my shoes!" said the voice.

"Your shoes?" asked Mack.

"But I found clues!" said the voice.

"Clues?" asked Mack. "What clues?"

"Look in the envelope on your doorstep!" said the voice.

"Redd," Mack called, "do you see an envelope on our doorstep?"

Redd opened the door. He peeked outside. "Sorry, Boss. No envelope. Just the morning paper."

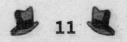

"Is this some kind of **prank**?" asked Mack. "There's no envelope here."

"But I left it at Number *12* Beach Street," said the voice in a panic.

"Well, there's your problem," said Mack. "Our office is Number *21* Beach Street. You must have—"

"Can't chat now," cried the voice. **"I'm on the move!"**

Click went the phone.

As a private eye, it wasn't unusual for Mack to get strange phone calls from morning until night. But this

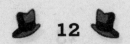 12

one was one of the strangest.

Mack took out his notebook. He **jotted** down a few questions.

> Who was that on the phone?
> What happened to the shoes?
> What is in the envelope?

Just then Redd called from the doorway. "Hey, Boss, take a look at this!"

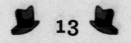

He held up the morning paper.

"How could the ants escape?"

asked Redd.

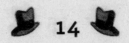

14

"They must have had help on the outside," said Mack.

Mystery phone calls?

Escaped ants?

Mack Rhino, Private Eye, needed to think. He did his best thinking at **Terry Berry**'s Smoothie Shack. "Next stop . . . ," he said.

"Fifi's Fine Furniture?" asked Redd.

"Soon," said Mack. "First, let's swing by Terry's."

3

Banana Supremes

Terry Berry's Smoothie Shack was Beach Street's favorite hangout. Large umbrellas shaded the tables. Mini umbrellas shaded the drinks.

Mack and Redd stepped up to the counter.

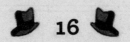

"Hi, guys," said Terry. "What can I get you today?"

"We'll have the usual," said Mack.

"Two Banana Supremes, coming right up," said Terry. "One jumbo. One mini."

"This place is really hopping today," said Redd.

"Everyone's here for the Big Race," said Terry. "Folks say this is going to be the biggest Big Race yet."

"I'm rooting for **Jackie Rabbit**," said Redd. "She's going to use the prize money for a new Beach Street playground."

"But she'll have to outrun **Skunks McGee**," said Terry. She handed Mack and Redd their drinks.

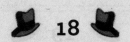

"Skunks McGee?" said Mack. "Wasn't he thrown out of last year's race for cheating?"

"That's the one," said Terry. "But he's being watched like a hawk this year. Plus, he promised to run fair. Maybe Skunks has changed his stripes."

Mack sipped his smoothie and studied the crowd along Beach Street.

There were the usual faces—**Surfer Jo**, **Lifeguard Sally**, and the **Juggling Jenkins Twins**. And

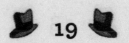 19

there was one not-so-usual face: a **hobbled** horse who wasn't very happy.

The horse wore a racing number for the Big Race. She also wore running shoes that barely stayed on her feet ... or hooves.

The horse **shuffled** up to the counter.

"Hey, why the long face?" asked Terry.

"It was the strangest thing," said the horse. "I went to put

on my running shoes, and **my laces were gone!** No Big Race for me today."

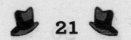

"Is that so?" asked Mack. He jotted this down in his notebook.

More shoe trouble? That was strange.

Maybe the envelope held a clue. Mack added this to his list:

Track down
that envelope.

He finished his smoothie. "Next stop ...," he said.

"Fifi's Fine Furniture?" asked

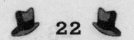

Redd hopefully. "You really need a new chair."

"Soon," said Mack. "First, we pay a visit to Number 12 Beach Street."

A Wild Goose Chase

Mack and Redd made their way down Beach Street.

Number 14 was Sam's Pots and Pans. Number 13 was Bella's Bikes and Bells. And Number 12 was . . .

"Would you take a look at

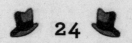

that," said Mack. "It's Queenie's Cupcakes."

"Lucky for us," said Redd. "We can pick up the envelope *and* two cupcakes. One jumbo. One mini."

"Good thinking," said Mack.

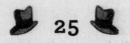

"I'll wait here and keep an eye out for anything unusual."

Mack sat down on a bench.

He saw a biker with a flat tire roll into Bella's Bikes and Bells.

He saw a chef with a pan walk out of Sam's Pots and Pans.

Nothing unusual.

In fact, the warm sunshine felt good on his horn.

Mack leaned back and closed his eyes. He thought about the very first case he and Redd had solved together: Case #1—A Wild

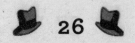

Goose Chase. That case had **ruffled** a few feathers.

A flock of geese had been missing one of its members. It turned out the goose had stopped at Queenie's cupcake shop while everyone else flew south.

Silly goose!

Mack felt something tapping on his horn.

"Have a nice **catnap**?" Redd giggled.

"I was just doing some thinking," said Mack. "Did you find the envelope?"

"It wasn't there," said Redd. "And neither was Queenie."

"Where did she go?" asked Mack.

"To get more flour, butter, and sugar," said Redd. "They were all out of cupcakes. A customer

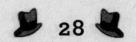

bought every last one early this morning."

"No more cupcakes?" said Mack. "In that case, next stop is ..."

"**Daisy**'s Blossom Barn!" said Redd.

"Huh?" asked Mack. "Why do we need flowers?"

"The cashier told me that today is Queenie's birthday," Redd replied.

Mack took out his notebook. He added this to his list:

Pick up flowers
for Queenie.

Then Mack stood up and ... fell
right out of his shoes!
"Leaping lizards!" cried
Mack. "Somebody swiped my
laces!"

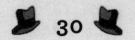

Two Victory Wreaths

Mack **lumbered** down Beach Street. Without laces in his shoes, he could only shuffle his feet. Redd followed close behind.

They opened the door to the colorful Blossom Barn.

"Hi, guys," said Daisy. "How can I help you?"

"We need some flowers," said Redd. "It's Queenie's birthday."

Daisy pointed to a row of beautiful **bouquets**. "Take your pick," she said.

Redd flew to the display. Mack shuffled behind.

"What happened to your shoes, Mack?" asked Daisy.

 33

"Some joker stole his laces," said Redd.

"Why would anyone do that?" asked Daisy.

"That's what we're trying to **untangle**," said Mack.

Redd picked out a bouquet and handed it to Daisy. "This one will be perfect," he said.

"Let me tie a ribbon on it," said Daisy. "And how about some ribbons for your shoes, Mack?"

"Thanks," said Mack. "I hope I can return the favor."

"Maybe you can," said Daisy. "I need someone to deliver these **victory wreaths** to the finish line for the winner."

Daisy pointed to two large wreaths. One was made of roses

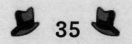 35

and lilies. The other was made of **skunk cabbage**.

"Why are there *two* victory wreaths?" asked Redd.

"The skunk cabbage is in case Skunks McGee wins the Big Race," said Daisy. "He hates the smell of flowers."

"Is that so?" said Mack. He jotted this down in his notebook.

Mack put one wreath over one arm and the other wreath over the other arm. Redd grabbed the bouquet for Queenie. They

 36

headed to the finish line.

Mack studied the crowd along Beach Street. There were the usual faces—Surfer Jo, Lifeguard Sally,

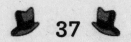

and the Juggling Jenkins Twins.

And one face they had been looking for—Queenie Zee. Mack and Redd hurried over to her.

"Happy birthday!" said Redd. He handed Queenie the bouquet.

"Thank you, Redd," said Queenie. "You're sweeter than a cupcake." Redd's cheeks blushed a little redder.

"And I have something for you, Mack," she said. "This envelope was left at my shop by mistake. Probably because I'm at Number 12 Beach Street and you're at—"

"Number 21 Beach Street," said Mack.

Queenie handed Mack the envelope.

"What's inside?" she asked.

"Clues, I hope," said Mack.

He opened the envelope. It was full of . . .

Crumbs?

Mack and Redd looked closer.

Cupcake crumbs?

"If I didn't know better," said Mack, "I'd say this had the Ant Hill Gang written all over it."

"But I thought they were at the ant farm upstate," said Queenie.

"Not anymore," said Mack. "They broke out last night."

"But it couldn't be them!" said Queenie. "I sold all the cupcakes to Skunks McGee this morning."

40

"*Skunks McGee?*" cried Redd. "*He's* the one who bought all the cupcakes?"

Queenie nodded. "He was very excited. In fact, he could barely stand still."

"Is that so?" said Mack. He jotted this down in his notebook.

Leader of the Pack

The crowd at the finish line was getting **restless**.

"Where are the runners?" asked Mack. "Shouldn't they be on Beach Street by now?"

Redd perched on Mack's horn

to get a better view. "Wait. I see someone," he said. "The leader is . . . *Skunks McGee*?"

He was the only runner in sight.

"But where's Jackie Rabbit?" asked Redd.

"Haven't you heard?"
said Surfer Jo. "Someone stole the laces out of her running shoes."

"And every runner is in the same pickle," said Lifeguard Sally. "Everyone but Skunks McGee, that is. He's sure to win now."

"You mean Skunks is the only runner with laces?" asked Mack.

"That's right," said the Jenkins Twins sadly. "It looks like we won't get a new playground."

"Something about this doesn't smell right," said Mack.

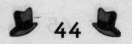

"It's probably the skunk cabbage," giggled Redd.

"Maybe," said Mack. "But I'll bet you that Skunks is up to his old tricks again."

Mack took out his notebook. He added this to his list:

Let Skunks McGee smell the roses.

Mack and Redd made their way to the front of the crowd.

"Hey, Skunks!" Mack called

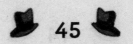

out. "Do you have time for an autograph?"

Skunks slowed down. He was still the only runner in sight. The prize money was as good as his.

"I guess I have time for a fan," said Skunks. Actually, Skunks was glad to take a break. This running was hard work.

"It looks like you're a **shoo-in** for first place," said Mack.

"You've got the Big Race all tied up," added Redd.

"I knew it from the start," said Skunks.

"I bet you did," said Mack. "In that case, we might as well give this to you now."

Mack placed one of the victory wreaths around Skunks. The one made of roses and lilies, that is.

"Flowers!" Skunks cried. He plugged his nose.

"I can't stand that stink!"

Coming Up Roses

Skunks didn't notice Jackie Rabbit shuffling past him until it was too late.

"Where did she come from?" Skunks cried. "I'm

supposed to win. I'm supposed
to get the prize money."

"Can't chat now," said Jackie.

"I'm on the move!"

Mack recognized that voice! It

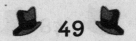

was the same voice that called the office this morning.

The crowd let out a huge roar as Jackie Rabbit shuffled across the finish line.

It wasn't a world record. But

Beach Street would get a new playground after all.

Mack presented her with the victory wreath. Even if it was made out of skunk cabbage, everything was coming up roses.

Skunks McGee sat in the middle of Beach Street, shaking his head.

"Well, there's always next year," he said.

"Not where you're going," said Mack. "I hear there's no Big Race at the ant farm upstate."

"*Ant farm?*" said Skunks. "What did I do?"

"*You* stole all the laces," said Mack.

"Now how would I do that?" asked Skunks. "Everyone was

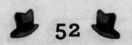 52

watching me like a hawk. Don't you think they would notice a skunk taking their laces?"

"He's got a point, Boss," said Redd.

Did Mack have it all wrong?

He took out his notebook and reviewed his notes.

Then the pieces fell into place like ants on a log.

"Skunks and the Ant Hill Gang are in cahoots!" said Mack.

"They're in what?" asked Redd.

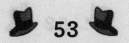 53

"They're working together," said Mack.

"So that explains why the ant farm escape caused such a big stink," said Redd. "Skunks was there to help them!"

"And it explains why Skunks couldn't stand still at Queenie's shop this morning," said Mack. "He had ants in his pants!"

Mack turned to Skunks. "You hired the ants to take the laces so you could win the Big Race."

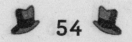 54

"And the prize money," said Redd.

"And all it cost me was some cupcakes," said Skunks slyly.

"But it didn't work," said Mack.

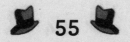

"Because I'm Mack Rhino, Private Eye. For cases sweet or stinky, I'm your guy. Or . . . rhino."

Another case closed.

Well, it was almost closed.

Ant Trap

Everyone gathered at Number 21 Beach Street to celebrate.

Mack studied the crowd. There were the usual faces—Surfer Jo, Lifeguard Sally, and the Juggling Jenkins Twins.

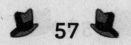

Daisy brought flowers. Terry brought Banana Supremes.

And Mack finally got one of Queenie's famous cupcakes. She brought a whole picnic basket full of them.

Jackie Rabbit arrived at the office with a very large box. On the outside it said FIFI'S FINE FURNITURE.

"This is for you," she said to Mack.

"For *me*?" said Mack.

"Of course," said Jackie. "I don't

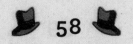

58

Rhino-Proof
Chair

expect you to work for free."

Mack opened the box.

"A rhino-proof chair!"

he said. "How did you ever know?"

Jackie Rabbit smiled at Redd

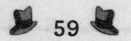

and said, "A little birdie told me."

"Well, it's been quite a day," said Mack. He took out his notebook and reviewed his list.

Blinds √
Sleeves √
Chocolate milk √
Get a rhino-proof chair. √
Track down
that envelope. √
Pick up flowers
for Queenie. √
Let Skunks McGee
smell the roses. √

"There's only one thing left to do," said Mack.

He added this to his list:

> Set an ant trap.

Mack and Redd borrowed Queenie's picnic basket. There were still a few cupcakes left.

Then they set the basket outside Number 21 Beach Street . . . and waited.

It didn't take long for the Ant Hill

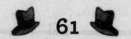

Gang to show up. The ants came marching one by one. They just couldn't resist Queenie's cupcakes.

Silly ants!

And Mack Rhino, Private Eye, could finally shut the lid on Case #100—The Big Race Lace Case.

"There's just one thing I don't get," said Redd. "Whatever happened to all those shoelaces?"

Word List

bouquet (boo·KAY): A bunch of flowers tied together

catnap (CAT·NAP): A short rest

compete (cum·PEET): Try to win or get something

evidence (EH·vi·dense): An item that proves something is true

hobbled (HAH·buld): Walking with difficulty

humdinger (hum·DING·er): Something exciting or special

jotted (JAH·ted): Wrote quickly

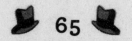 65

lumbered (LUM·bird): Moved slowly and clumsily

prank (PRANK): A trick or practical joke

restless (REST·less): Uneasy or not at rest

reviewed (ree·VYOOD): Studied or looked over carefully

ruffled (RUH·fuld): Made a mess of; upset

shoo-in (SHOO·in): Certain to win

shuffled (SHUH·fuld): Took short steps and dragged one's feet

skunk cabbage (SKUNK CA·bidge): A plant that has a strong smell like a skunk

snaked (SNAYKD): Followed a curved or twisting path

untangle (un·TANG·gul): Untwist or solve

victory wreaths (VICK·tor·ee REETHS): Flowers in the shape of a circle used as a trophy or prize

Questions

1. At the beginning of the story, Mack gets a strange phone call. Who is the mystery caller?

2. How does Skunks McGee plan to win the Big Race?

3. Why is Jackie Rabbit's victory wreath made out of skunk cabbage?

4. How do Mack and Redd finally trap the Ant Hill Gang?

5. Mack Rhino uses a notebook to record his thoughts and ideas. Do you use a notebook or journal? What kinds of notes do you write in it?

LOOKING FOR A FAST, FUN READ?
BE SURE TO MAKE IT ALADDIN QUIX!

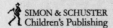